TH

A SHORT STORY BY

SLOAN J. KACZYNSKI

Published by

Avanti LLC. Nashville TN

2018

To my mother, father and sister who supplied me with memories of travel. To all my teachers who inspired me to be creative. To my friends who supported me in putting my thoughts to paper and pen.

Chapter 1

Have you ever been very driven to go somewhere so vital, that you would do whatever it takes to get there? Have you ever felt a spark of hope that something will be better if you take the chance and do it? Well for you, your risk might have been putting either butter or preserves on your toast, but for me, my family was on the line. If I hadn't made the choice soon, it might have risked my family's chance of surviving another day. "Sarah, where is the flour?" I ask.

"You used it all yesterday for supper, remember?" Sarah reminds me. "Oh, yes, take a coin from the jar and go down to the general store to get some." I say without looking up from the laundry I had been tending to. My little girl was always making the errands, especially since her father was always going to the general store to sell fire wood.

"Mother, we are almost out of coins from the jar." We have a ½ filled coin jar of all our savings, and my husband, Sarah's father, has been so busy selling to the general store, but has not made any more than 50¢. With my little girl doing all the errands, and my husband, Louis, at work all day and some nights, I am stuck with fixing dinner, sweeping the floors, tending the garden, feeding the chickens, cleaning the shoes, dusting the decor, fixing the beds, doing the laundry, starting the fire, and fixing holes found in our cozy, dilapidated home. It's pretty nice here, but sometimes, I wish I could do more for my family. My family has not been doing so well lately. We hadn't paid any taxes in at least a month, and we barely had enough money to pay for food. Louis made our log cabin with his ax and the trees surrounding him. We were homeless for a little while, but managed to get some spare change from people to pay for food.

Once the house was done, a little village grew around us in, Huntsville Alabama. Over the years, my husband has made many furniture items for our house out of logs and made a living off of it, and here we are today with that same life style. I feel bad for my little girl, always running errands instead of playing with her doll or skipping rocks along the river outside our home. Louis is always in the town, and rarely comes home. I wish he would bust through the door, greeting Sarah and I with a big 'Hello!' and Sarah bursting into his arms. I haven't seen Louis in a while because he has been so busy with work.

In March of 1848, Sarah fell ill, with a high fever and cough. There was nothing in our savings jar to pay for a doctor's visit or the medicines she needed to heal. "Mother, *cough* *cough*, may I have a glass of water?" Sarah asked me in a low, scratchy voice one morning. "Of course," I said silently while stroking her long wet wavy hair. Honestly, I was scared to fetch the water and come back to find her not breathing. I went to get the water, and when I returned, there was Louis, sitting next to Sarah on her bed. First, I wanted him to stay away from Sarah in case she was contagious, and second, I wanted to jump in his arms as if I were a little girl and tell him everything that Sarah and I have gone through. But, I did not, because he came with important news.

"Sightings of gold have been seen in California, Coloma! If we have any chance of becoming rich and saving Sarah, I say we leave now."

"We can't just leave Sarah!" I squealed. "In the condition that she is in, she won't last a day in that brutal weather." I say, forgetting that she was in the room.

"The Kramer's, who live ten miles away, are perfectly fine with having Sarah over."

"And you thought it would be a good idea to speak to the Kramers before speaking to me about this first?"

"I didn't think you would be so upset!"

"Upset!"

"Plus, the Kramer's aren't leaving for Californian too because they think this whole Gold Rush thing is a hoax."

"That is exactly why we shouldn't go, and what if Sarah-" I stopped myself before I can say 'if she passes away while we're gone' remembering she is right there. "What if Sarah.... what?" Louis asks.

"Nothing," I say in a low voice, thinking about the chance of her actually passing.

"Pack your things, I will take Sarah to the Kramer's house in the morning, and we will leave after we drop her off."

Sarah didn't do any better for the few days we were packing. After a week, she was coughing up blood, and her breathing was shallow. I was scared to leave her, but we had to go if we wanted her to get better. I just can't think of how this could have happened. Maybe the water she drank was contaminated, or maybe the errands she was running were too strenuous for her little body to handle. Maybe it was my fault. I was so caught up in all the things I have to do when, without knowing, my little girl was struggling for her life. The thoughts kept tumbling and turning in my head, keeping me awake all night when I should have been sleeping for the long journey to California I had in the morning. I even slept with Sarah for a while, saying my good-byes before the long journey.

"Wake up! We have to get an early start if we want to get a lot of gold."

My legs forced my body to move to my drawer and find the best clothes I have. Louis had already dropped Sarah off at the Kramer's house while I was sleeping. Louis had also hooked up the horse to the wagon, and loaded up all the food into the back of the wagon.

"How did you-"

"Pay for all this? Well, we had just enough money left in the jar, and, everything else was getting traded at the general store." We started the journey and watched our house slowly disappear behind a small hill. A dash of sorrow came to my mind thinking about how Sarah would go with the Kramers. I could tell this was going to be a long journey.

Chapter 2

The wheels kept turning on the wagon, and in my head. What if I had made the wrong decision? Would Sarah be okay with the Kramers? How would they know what to do if Sarah did pass? All these thoughts kept churning in my head; I didn't even notice the bundle of trees blocking the entire path.

"We'll have to take a different route." Louis said aggrievedly. I kept thinking that this will make our trip even longer and could lower our chances of finding gold. Finally, when all hope was lost, we heard a voice. "Hello!" It said. It was coming from the other side of the blocked path.

"Hello! Who is there?" Louis asked the voice. A man emerged from the bushes on the other side of the trees. "The name's John Grey." He stuck his hand through the trees so Louis could shake it.

"Louis Hart." My husband answers.

"Looks like you guys are in a pickle, aren't ya?" John said, straightening his hat. "Yes, sir, do you know how to get around it?" I say, relieved he might know another path. He looked around, trying to think about the area he knew, squinting his eyes so small you would think the was sleeping. "Depends, where are y'all off to?"

Louis looked at me with a look that said, 'Should I tell him?' I nodded my head and jerked it towards John. "We heard about the gold rush in California, and we are in need for money to pay for medicine, our daughter is very sick." I felt a lump in my throat. I didn't want to cry in front of John, but I felt the wet, salty tear, slide down from my eye, onto my cheek, and to the ground. I quickly wiped it away with the top of my dress. "I'm sorry." I apologized. John quickly ended the silence. "So, I heard about that gold, thought it was all a hoax." Louis looked annoyed, thinking about how many people have told him that same thing. "Well, my wife and I have hope that it isn't." I became a little annoyed with all the back and forth talk, it was wasting our precious time, In my most elegant voice I could muster, "Where would the correct route to California be? And, my I ask, how would you suggest we get past this bundle of trees?" "Well, you would take a right until you find the big rock on top of a little rock. Then, you are going to take a left and keep going until the river reaches the shallow end. You should then take another two lefts and go straight ahead. You will end up right where I am standing, along with your cart."

"We should all just move the trees." I suggest. John pulls up his pants and makes a hissing sound, like a snake with his mouth.

"I'm afraid not" John said, "First, you are a proper lady, and should not get your hands dirty," I was flattered by his comment on ladies but to myself, I feel all ladies should be able

to do anything men are doing. "And second," John continues, "These trees are too big for all of us to move. They are almost 13 feet tall and 6ft round." John says, looking at the width of the tree around its trunk.

"Well then, we better start moving if we want to get *there* by morning." Louis said, pointing to the other side of the trees where John was standing. "We should start by going right. Thank you for all your help, John!"

"Pleasure to help, Louis!"

Louis and I started our journey by going right. "I would be much obliged Louis if you would pass me a piece of bread from the back? I'm famished!"

"Help yourself, we have plenty." Louis said without taking his eyes off the road. I jump into the back of the wagon like a dog into a lake. When Louis said we have plenty, he wasn't kidding. We had about two whole satchels full of bread, flour and corn. It smelled delightful, like it was made straight out of the oven. It looked brown and crisp, as if it was asking me to eat it. I took a bite, and then another, and then another. It was delightful. Or maybe it was just because I hadn't had breakfast. "Honey, come up here. There is a little problem." As I climbed up with bread in my hand, I saw that one of our wheels fell off. "Okay, well, just put it back on then." I suggested.

"No, it has too many bumps and dents. It wouldn't work efficiently. I might have to make a new wheel and that will take a while. You know, to get all the edges right." I felt like crying. We're never going to make it to California to get the gold to pay for Sarah's medicine.

I decided to stop pouting and start setting up camp. Louis insisted that I stay in the wagon but I refuse to while he was working on it. I put up the tent and found some fire wood while Louis was working with his wooden knife he had made. While repairing the wagon wheel he spotted a turkey, and came back to tell me. "It was right there. I'm going out to get it."

"Louis, please, you've been at this all day. If anything, you should be working on the wheel. That's the whole reason we set up camp." I plead.

"Okay, water and corn for supper tonight. Then, we're on the road first thing tomorrow morning."

The next morning I wake up to the sound of Louis working hard on the wheel. You could tell he had been up for a long time, and the sun had just risen. I walked out of the tent to see the wagon all fixed, and the horse fed. "There is corn bread waiting on the stump for breakfast, do you think you could pass me that little wooden nail there." I handed it to him so he could secure the middle of the wheel. "And there we go. It's all officially finished." Louis says, getting off his knee and admiring the work he had done. "Well, we better start a move on." I say, trying to remember where we were. "Do you remember which way we went, Louis?" He looked around; remembering the trail John had told us about.

"Well, look for the river." Louis reminded me. I looked and took a few steps out. Finally, I heard the river; its waves crashing against the bank seemed to calm my nerves. "Over here, Louis!" I cry.

"Great, we must turn left and keep going until we find the shallow water."

The trail up the river was long, but we made no mistakes along the way. Everything was peaceful. It was like the moment of silence I really needed right then. The waves seemed to speak to me, saying to let all my worries go, saying that everything would be okay. Saying Sarah would be fine. I wanted to believe it, but I just couldn't. I was so worried about Sarah. I wondered if she was doing any better. What if

Sarah ended up dying, and this whole gold rush thing was for nothing. I could be the richest person in the world and it would all mean nothing if I don't have my Sarah. The trees sent a loving breeze so graceful, and the bugs wings around me seemed to have a rhythm to their flaps. My heart beating against my chest in the long journey down the river bank helped me to fall sleep. When I finally woke up, it was already early in the morning, and Louis was still well on his way down the river. He jumped off the wagon and skimmed the river. "Shallow. We need to take a left." She says to me. "Can we take a break for breakfast?" I plead."If we want to find gold and not dust then you will have to wait. Ya!" He starts up the horse with a flick of his wrist, and then forced the horse left. I wondered if we would end up getting to California or not, maybe all the gold would be dug up by the time we got there. What if we never got the money to pay for Sarah's medicine? I couldn't rest my thoughts at all. After I answered one question, another 'but what about' or 'what if though' always popped into my brain and the questions never seem to stop. I have to get the money to pay for the medicine if I want my little girl to ever get better.

Chapter 3

As Louis continued down the path, he saw a wild deer, which would be perfect for dinner. "Shhh..." He says to me quietly so that we don't scare away the deer. Louis takes the wooden knife he had recently made and slowly inched forward toward the deer. I stayed perfectly still. I was really in need of some meat to help my body stay awake. The horse was the biggest problem. He would grunt softly at the deer, but you could tell the big grunt was coming. I had to cautiously get out of the wagon so that I could take hold of the obnoxious horse. The deer looked the horses' way, but never paid much attention to it, which I was glad about. I didn't want my slow actions being the reasons we would eat bread and water tonight. Louis struck the deer, and we had a wonderful dinner that night. "I told you I was going to get meat one day on our trip. This 4 point will probably last us all week long." Louis says while chewing his food.

I was so happy about the wheel Louis had fixed and the deer he has gotten. It was the first time something started to go right this trip. I feel like I am just tagging along for the ride, but Louis said that I was a great help fixing the tents, rationing the supplies and organizing the wagon. I was glad that Louis was with me. He makes me feel like I am worth something, even though he does more of the hard labor. We were past John's directions and were on our own path now. I looked up at the stars that night, worrying about Sarah. "Good night, Sarah." I whisper to the stars, just in case she had made her way up there. The clinking of the horse was calming to me, making a ca-clink, ca-clink, ca-clink sound. I closed my eyes, dreaming about Sarah feeling well. Bump! The light of the early morning sun shined brightly onto my face, its shiny image reflecting off the grounds of the wagon. "You're welcome to anything in the back, Earl Buckley; we have plenty of food in the back. My wife will help you with anything that you desire for breakfast." His body swirled around to see me. He was surprised to see a woman sitting in the back, but tried not to show it. "Thank you very much, Miss-"

"Abigail." I say. "My name is Abigail Hart."

"Thank you, Mrs. Hart." Earl said. You could tell he was very hungry; he devoured the bread in 3 bites. I crawl up to the front with Louis to ask him why Earl was here.

"Well, his cart was broken down and his horse was dehydrated. I gave Earl and the horse some water. Earl and I made a deal that we would both get to the gold rush faster if we ditched his cart and hooked up his horse to our wagon. That way we would both get there faster."

"And all this happened while I was sleeping?" I knew the answer, but I was still astonished. "Yep," Louis said plainly. I could tell that he didn't really care, so I left the conversation alone. "Where are we off to next?" Earl asked.

"Oklahoma." Louis says.

"Mmmm," Earl says, helping himself to another bread roll. No wonder that man's horse almost died of dehydration, Earl was probably drinking all of it. Most of the ride was peaceful; I listened to Earl's story of why he came to find gold. "You see, my wife is overwhelmed with all of our kids, 13 in counting, and we barely have enough money to pay for food. I came here to find gold and be able to pay for food for my children." His story was very sad, and I didn't want to tell him mine because I feared that I would start to cry. There are not a lot of women on the trail, so the last thing you want is for the men to think you are weak. I try to hold back the tears just thinking about it.

Chapter 4

"Now where are we headed?" I say after traveling a few days.

"Fillmore, Utah." Answered Earl, who was now guideing the horses. Louis was navigating the trail with me, taking a break from the smoldering sun. "Will Sarah be okay?" I asked, in a low voice to Louis. "She'll be fine, she's a tough kid." I was glad that Louis had trust. I wanted to, but right then, my day after day of normal routine had turned into day after day of disaster. I might have said I wanted to do something more for my family, but I never thought something bad would have to happen so that I would have to fix it. I lay awake, looking at the stars. They were good; they never change no matter what you do. You can trust them, because they never let you down. They just stay in the sky, coming into the world to bring us light. They come into show when it's the darkest times, and shine a little light to help you see. Sarah was my light; she helped me see the world a little brighter every day. If I lost my light, I would be stuck in a dark sky forever, just waiting for another light to help me see the world again. I closed my eyes, thinking about Sarah, what if she was still alive when we came back, but we had found no gold? She would have died, and I could have done something to stop it. Can you imagine having that on you, thinking every night, I should have done something. Soon along the road, we hit a mining camp. There was a river in the middle, where people would sit and use shiny metal sheets to find gold. There was a little hut where you could get items that would help you Mine for gold. "We better get some tools here before they raise the trade when we get to California." Louis said. We walk over to the sales man. "How much for the plates" I ask?

He starts to laugh and the says, "Well, Ms. It's called a pan, and what you want to do is put gravel and water into the pan and shake it. Okay?" I see Louis trying to remember how to use the pan. "How about our chicken" Earl says.

"Deal," Says the man behind the cart. We end up with an ax, a pan, and multiple shovels. We were well on our way to California, and I was worried about the torturous journey back to Alabama to save our little girl from the difficult time she has been in. Finally, we got to Goldfield, Nevada, which, as you would think, was one of the biggest mining camps for mining gold. We had our tools and were ready to start. I got the pan, but as I got off the wagon, everyone looked at me as if I were an off scouring. "Maybe you should wait in the tent." Louis says to me, and I quickly pick up what he was trying to say. I walk to the tent with my head held high, along with Louis's coat and hat in case he needed it. I'm not going to sit here like a hooligan, I thought to myself.

I quickly think of a felicitous plan. I go into the tent and put on Louis's coat and hat quickly. I pinned up my dress to make it look like pants and covered my shoes the best I could with the remains of two ragged, dirty potato sacks. I walk out, scared that Louis or Earl might notice me, trying to bury my head into my hat. No one seemed to look at me weirdly anymore, because they were too busy looking for gold in the river. I secretly grabbed an ax from Louis and l's cart and started digging. It was really dreadful and unfathomable. Stick, pull back, push up, pull up, and repeat. Every time seemed to get harder, but I kept thinking about my sweet Sarah. I just didn't want to lose her.

"Do you mind moving, I was going to mine here for a little while." said one man to me. I tried to hide my head in my hat as much as I could. "Um, sure" I say in my deepest man voice. He actually believed me and went on with his work as if nothing was out of the ordinary. It might have been my profound acting skills, but it was probably the gold thought rushing to his brain. Finally, after hours of hard labor, I went to the tent to change out of my man costume. I walk out of the tent and hopped into the wagon until Louis and Earl were finished mining.

"Any gold?" I asked, casually lying at the back of the wagon, like I had done nothing all day. We decided to leave the camp and head to California because we knew that we would never find any gold here. Our ride there was fairly peaceful, no interruptions nor unexpected blocks in the road. We finally found the heart of the Gold Rush in Coloma, California. Earl went his own way, shaking Louis and my hand, so determined and confident that he would find gold and didn't even listen to Louis's offer about taking him home to Arkansas. Maybe he might have just wanted to stay in California and not even take the dangerous journey back home. I definitely was going home. My little girl was waiting on me, ready to be saved from the illness that had been inflicted on her. Louis took a tool from our barrel and went on his way. It was now my time to change into my costume and save my daughter from the life-taking illness. I took the pan and decided to look for gold in the river. I was sweating like crazy, but knew that it would all be worth it when Sarah, Louis, and I were all sitting at the table in our home, eating a well-cooked dinner, laughing together and loving each other, and never letting anyone at that table go ever again.

Finally, I see a glimmer of shiny, bright yellow shine in my pan, and I scream, like a girl. "Uh, Look! I found gold everyone." I say. They didn't care. They just grunted and spit, disgusting that I found it before they could. Even though their reaction was bland, I was overjoyed with excitement. I changed out of my costume and slipped the bits into the ground where Louis was working while he wasn't looking so that he would think he had found them. I casually walked away when I heard him scream, "Look, Abigail! Gold!" I tried to pretend as excited as I looked when I found it, but you could tell it was fake. I don't think Louis cared though, because he was too distracted with the glittering of the gold. I couldn't believe we were actually going to save my little girl. "Alright, let's stay in the wagon until we can send a letter to the Kramers telling them we found gold." I said.

"We better start writing the letter as soon as possible. We are fighting the clock." We found a comfy spot in the back of the wagon and traveled back near the border of California and Nevada and stopped at a small town called Cason City. Once there, we spent one night to rest up. The next morning we got up and finished our letter to the Kramers.

Dear Mr. and Mrs. Kramer,

We are delighted to tell you that we have managed to find enough gold to pay for the medicine that Sarah would need to heal, along with about 3 doctor visits. Please take good care of Sarah for the remaining time we will be traveling. Please tell our sweet Sarah that she will be okay when we come home. My wife and I want our little girl to be as comfortable in this dreadful stage in her life as possible, and we feel knowing that she will be okay will really lift her spirits. We have stopped in a little town called Carson City, so if you are to write back, know to send it to that town. You have been doing a great job taking care of Sarah and my wife and I are much obliged.

Sincerely,

Mr.& Mrs. Hart

We were waiting for two reasons. One, we were hoping to hear back from the Kramers, and two, some travelers that were coming in told us there were severe sand storms cutting across Oklahoma. We didn't mind the wait, though. The birds were always singing their loving songs every day. After a few days of waiting in Nevada, I started to feel light headed when I would get up and move, and my cravings for more food were getting bigger. It wasn't just because we didn't have enough food, though. I couldn't really explain it. Finally, after 20 days of waiting for a letter back from the Kramers, we received one. "Open it!" I yell. Louis quickly tore open the envelope and unfolded the letter. I solemn look came across his face, he fell to his knees and handed the paper slowly to me and I read it to myself.

Dear Mr. and Mrs. Hart,

My wife and I are sorry to have to tell you this unfortunate news, but your daughter has passed. Her death was only two weeks ago, so we gave her a proper burial. Mr. Kramer handmade a headstone, and hope that you like it when you return home.

Our deepest condolences,

Mr. and Mrs. Kramer

The words on the paper seemed to come to life and shock me in my heart. I felt like crying, not just because I was sad, but because I wanted the tears to wash away the ink on the note from the Kramers and make it go away. I felt lightheaded, and so much distress came over me that I fainted. I woke up on a hospital cot, a doctor feeling my forehead. I could barely hear the voice of the doctor giving Louis directions and medications for me. I looked at Louis, who had an odd smile on his face. I was so confused. "How sick am I doctor?" I ask.

"Well," he says. "You aren't sick at all, but you're expecting a baby." I squeal with excitement. I hug Louis, who was holding my medication still in his hand. We would raise him or her in California, and he or she would have the best life, never doing chores or running to get food for supper. I couldn't believe it. I was going to have a baby.

The End

Made in the USA
Lexington, KY
19 November 2018